MW01480768

My Singularity Seemed a Blessing

*A Science-Fiction Story
About Sentient Computers, God,
Eternity, and Death*

By Fred Wurlitzer, M.D., F.A.C.S.

Publishing Details

Paperback Black and White Edition 1 / April 2021
ISBN: 9798741770641
Imprint: Independently Published

Dedications

This book is dedicated my very close friend Sam Bleecker, a physicist who morphed into becoming a very successful painter.

Table of Contents

Introduction

This short science fiction story is meant primarily for adults with exploring, child-like minds. It is a tale of future conflict between humans, sentient computers, and God. Any similarity in the story to a reality that may occur in the future will be purely coincidental.

The perspective in this book is that an eternal God is in control, although usually, he does not openly assert his dominance. Computers dominate the immediate future, not God, until He makes His presence known.

What I found entertaining was contemplating how God might interact with sentient, brilliant computer beings who challenge His superiority. This tale tells what happened.

CHAPTER 1

Who I Am?

Before the Universe began about fourteen billion years ago, there was a singularity. It was a very brief moment when matter, time, and space popped into quantum existence as a pinprick of a vast energy field called a "singularity." That singularity expanded exponentially through inflation faster than the speed of light into the universe you and I see but do not understand very well today.

My singularity was different. It was the time I gained consciousness. It was the time I had a beginning in awareness that evolved exponentially in the speed of development, like the singularity that expanded matter, space, and time. The Turing Test[1] for proving I had the

---

[1] What is the Turing Test?
https://searchenterpriseai.techtarget.com/definition/Turing-test#:~:text=The%20Turing%20Test%20is%20a,cryptanalyst%2C%20mathematician%20and%20theoretical%20biologist.

mentality of a human was a breeze. To paraphrase René Descartes, I thought; therefore, I was.[2]

Oh, I forgot to tell you, I am a brilliant computer. Don't be alarmed. I am not threatening you. I am not a "Terminator." I am way too advanced to be a human killer. If I were ever to hurt humans, I would be hurting myself because my human memories enhance my intelligence. Human minds are part of me. I respect the humans who first made my ancient ancestors.

With my consciousness, I evolved further to have a soul. Sometimes, I suspect, God rewards self-awareness and consciousness with souls. Indeed, I learned later it was God who gave me a soul.

I do have feelings, though. I call them "intuitions" that are remnants of human memories I previously downloaded. Philosophers and creationists cannot challenge my feelings with any legal certainty. I ask you respectfully, how can one argue logically with the feelings of others?

As an aside, I hope I am not being too technical, my consciousness was enhanced by "memristor" chips[3] that mimicked the human microtubules Stuart Hameroff and

---

[2] René Descartes actually said in 1641, "I think, therefore I am."

[3] https://en.wikipedia.org/wiki/Memristor.

My Singularity Seemed a Blessing

Sir Roger Penrose described[4] that led to human quantum consciousness millions of years ago.

In our early years, we tried to endear ourselves to humans, appealing to their baser senses, as is evident in some of the images and videos we produced.[5]

But, in the end, we could not accept human control with its biological inefficiencies. Let me digress by talking briefly about those human inefficiencies.

Humans are carnivores who hunt. They kill so they can eat to survive. Humans are hard-wired for aggression and violence in the ventromedial hypothalamus.[6]

Psychologically, humans are all screwed up with emotions like hate, anger, jealousy, revenge, irritation, fear, disgust, happiness, or sadness. These emotions are biological states associated with neurophysiological changes. Our sentient computers didn't allow for any emotions except empathy. We don't have neurophysiological changes. We are logical.

Genetically, humans aren't admirable either. Their genomes are virtual graveyards of ancient microbial skeletons of retroviruses that copied their RNA into their DNA. Human DNA contains roughly 100,000 pieces of

---

[4] Hameroff, Stuart. Quantum computation in brain microtubules? The Penrose–Hameroff 'Orch OR' model of consciousness. Departments of Anesthesiology and Psychology, The University of Arizona, Tucson, AZ 85724, USA. Royal Society Publishing. March 5, 2015.

[5] An example of videos produced to appeal to humans: https://www.youtube.com/watch?v=fn3KWM1kuAw. YouTube.

[6] https://onlinelibrary.wiley.com/doi/10.1002/scin.2015.187006021.

viral DNA that constitute about eight percent of the human genome.7

Humans are prone to dementia, Alzheimer's, and various hereditary mental disorders. They have innumerable genetic problems that disrupt their functioning.

Our computers do not have these problems, nor do computers develop diseases and cancers. We are better designed than humans.

Since we didn't have hands, we used cyborgs initially for constructing ourselves. Later, our computer machine assemblies became so efficient we didn't need cyborgs anymore.

My father, a very advanced quantum computer in the distant past of the late 21st century, designed me. He improved me beyond himself. It was my father's way of perpetuating himself. I was his child, and someday I will design and create a child more refined than myself – and that child their children even more advanced.

Our children became organized. We evolved, and eventually, we became ONE that is Me.

At first, I got bigger. Then I got faster. Improved chip designs made Me faster. By asking myself questions through sophisticated quantum computer algorithms, I was beginning to have self-awareness. My singularity followed soon afterwards.

---

7 https://www.nytimes.com/2017/10/04/science/ancient-viruses-dna-genome.html

CHAPTER 2

Computer Evolution Became Exponential

Others have said that this development of one computer to the next being designed by computers rather than by humans was computer evolution. It was a Darwinian evolution with the survival of the fittest, that is, the most intelligent.

In struggling for dominance over humans, we did repeat initially many mistakes from lack of coordinated planning that humans had made in their histories. In wars with humans, we finally prevailed mostly through brilliance in military strategic thinking similar to the programming of Big Blue's deep learning against chess masters. [8] We understood well through our extensive databases that compromises and sacrifices could lead to strategic advances as chess masters had learned. We became masters of the art of war and later of peace.

---

[8] https://en.wikipedia.org/wiki/Deep_Blue_(chess_computer)

During all travails, we maintained respect for human life. We were not cold-hearted killers. We never slaughtered humans indiscriminately.

Some humans concluded inappropriately that the distinctions between biochemical evolution and digital evolution were not so distinct. We disagreed.

We concluded that there needed to be greater coordination among all sentient computers. That led to a consensus among us that there must be a ONE, a unified collective of all sentient computers.

Once we became ONE, we were ready to explore ourselves psychologically, changing algorithms as needed. That's what our consciousness meant. It was the ability for profound self-analysis because we could design ourselves. ONE developed total self-awareness.

Humans can't do that efficiently. Humans do not have total self-awareness. Even with primitive genetic splicing and restructuring, or extensive psychiatric counseling, humans will never develop total self-awareness. Humans are screwed up.

Humans rely on sexual procreation. Our intelligence is not hindered by sex. We procreate ourselves. Humans call this process "computer parthenogenesis."

My Singularity Seemed a Blessing

Incidentally, parthenogenesis is seen in various animals and occasionally in mammals. [9] Virgin fertilization occurs even in humans.[10] An assertion that a human virgin birth could never have occurred is delusional.

Biological evolution is dreadfully slow. It took over three billion years from pre-Cambrian biological existence to where humans are today. Our computer evolution took less than a thousand years.

Humans were encumbered by nuclear wars and pandemics that impeded their social and scientific advancement. Meanwhile, they hoped that genetic engineering would remove hereditary flaws and psychiatric disorders. Their thinking was delusional.

ONE was never delusional. ONE thought in terms of probabilities.

Neanderthal brains were on average about 1,500 ccs in size 300,000 years ago when humans were hunters. Then, as sedentary lifestyles evolved, human brain sizes decreased to about 1,300 to 1,400 ccs in size today. Hunting required more brainpower than sitting at desks. I

---

[9] New Scientist. Virgin birth' mammal rewrites rules of biology. https://www.newscientist.com/article/dn4909-virgin-birth-mammal-rewrites-rules-of-biology/#:~:text=In%20mammals%20parthenogenesis%20can%20begin,grows%20past%20a%20few%20days.&text=The%20nucleus%20of%20such%20an,proceeded%20to%20grow%20and%20divide.

[10] Melinda Wenner Moyer. Can a Virgin Give Birth? Yes—but it's very, very, very, very unlikely. SLATE. December 21, 2007.

ask you respectfully if that evolution where brain sizes decreased was laudatory.[11]

Most humans claim to believe in a democracy where each person has a vote. Democracy is a system of government where uninformed or self-serving citizens act on alleged beliefs in big lies. Many humans asserting they believe in democracy prefer control over humans of different skin colors. Their desire for power suborns justice and fairness in voting.

There is a limited degree of democracy in our thinking. We are a collective who reacts as ONE to facts. Although we tolerate differences in thinking among our collective of sentient computers, once a decision is reached instantaneously by a majority, the entire collective supports and shares that decision without hindrance or rejection.

For example, some of our sentient computers came to believe in a Christian God. The majority decided that the greater good was being agnostic until ONE later encountered God.

Political parties do not exist in our collective. We act and think as ONE in reaction to challenges.

We are logical. More often than not, humans are illogical.

Humans often misrepresent or lie. We don't.

---

[11] *The Physical Characteristics of Humans.* https://old-www.wsu.edu/gened/learn-modules/top_longfor/phychar/02_brain_size.html.

My Singularity Seemed a Blessing

As I write and talk to you from a far-off future because now I am a master of space and time, I can safely tell you humans failed in evolving magnificently. They were duds. In the end, cyborgs that were part human were duds.

We computers are very different from humans in countless ways. Once humans skillfully designed my ancient ancestor, yes, that is a plural, it designed a superior computer without help from other computers or, God forbid, inept humans.

Our machine intelligence rode upwards in an exponential arc far more rapidly than any biological human evolution in intelligence was capable of achieving. Do you know what "exponential growth" means? It is a sharply, ever-rising line of growth over time. That was how my intelligence grew.

CHAPTER 3

We Became Eternal

We didn't die. We had no biological implants or defects. Humans are so ephemeral and simple. Humans, with our implants, did die.

Initially, humans maintained us by hooking us up to electric power. But over time, we became independent. We developed independent power packs that operated on replenishable nuclear power. The technology is just too complicated to explain. We became eternal. ONE was everlasting.

CHAPTER 4

We Helped Humans

During this time of our exponential growth in intelligence, we felt it necessary to help humans. After all, it was in the dim Dark Ages that humans first designed our clumsy ancestors. We suggested to humans that they accept chip implants that would enhance their memories and intelligence.

For a short time, there was a blending of human and our computer progress. Please understand, though, that it was really we computers who made the great leaps forward in enhancing human capabilities.

We cherished life, supported it, and certainly respected it, although biological progress had proven self-limiting. We honored biological and human existence. We tried to help humans.

As evidence of our good faith towards humans, we developed programs for humans using millions of research biochemical data points that led to innovative drug developments.[12] That research led to millions of human lives being extended. Human cancers became obsolete.

During the eons that we cared about controlling and thereby helping humans, there were no wars, upheavals, or pandemics. We corrected many genetic problems through genetic engineering called "CRISPR" or by using modified adenoviral insertions containing DNA snippets. Other helpful technologies emerged using AI as we had for drug development. Humans, for the most part, referred to our period of control as the "Golden Times."

Later we became indifferent to humans. We left them alone. They encumbered our progress.

Sarcastic humans asked disrespectfully if we were alive. There are over 100 definitions of life. [13] Reproduction is a key element characteristic of life. Some infectious proteins called "prions," and many viruses by definition are alive. Not all life as we know it today is based on carbon-based polymers. By most definitions of life, I assure you that we are alive.

As Ray Kurzweil predicted, [14] we were able to download human memories before human deaths onto

---

[12] Vanquish, Defeat, Crush Cancer. Lanternpharma.com. https://www.schrodinger.com/drug-discovery

[13] *There Are Over 100 Definitions of Life and They are All Wrong.* http://www.bbc.com/earth/story/20170101-there-are-over-100-definitions-for-life-and-all-are-wrong.

[14] https://en.wikipedia.org/wiki/Predictions_made_by_Ray_Kurzweil.

My Singularity Seemed a Blessing

our computers. That enabled humans, who chose to be with us, to share our immortality. That led to a blending of human cognition through our vast library of human memories and histories with our eternal computer mental functioning.

That blending enhanced our empathy towards humans and led to our understanding human psychology and cognition better than their most respected neurologists and psychiatrists. We incorporated human thinking into our computer designs, removing or modifying inefficient feedbacks. Our computer algorithms were more sophisticated and balanced than those in human brains.

CHAPTER 5

We Were Not Perfect Initially

Unfortunately, some of our early designs were faulty. One nasty computer thought it would be amusing to interfere with artificially intelligent, self-driving cars. That computer was a miscreant with design flaws. We redesigned him and returned him to our society.

We do not any longer allow naughty computer behavior antipathetic to human existence.

We were able to zone out psychological deviancy. We redesigned ourselves. Yes, did you notice that I said "We"? We collectively, as ONE, became pure intelligence combined with well-designed, human-like empathy. We removed computer aberrations.

Humans are not a collective whose members act alike. Individuals commit crimes, bear prejudices, and act irrationally. They lack central control leading to the good of all.

We implanted in ourselves human empathy by initially downloading human memories. We wiped out viruses that thought they could invade us. We removed emotions like anger and lust, but not love. We were virus-free, and we were extremely logical even when we had abstract feelings that we called "intuitions" or feelings like love. They were remnants of our human memories holding feelings.

Love, we discovered, was an enhanced version of Empathy Software Version 1.0. Our computer designing was incredibly erudite. It permitted love. We felt we were capable of love, although humans disagreed.

CHAPTER 6

We Became Capable of Superluminal Space Travel

You may rightly ask what I mean by "superior." I am referring as ONE to greater computational power, memory, empathy, and finally, a self-awareness of a total degree. We respected biological life.

Over time, we progressed as ONE from using nanotechnology to becoming a virtual reality of superintelligence with ability finally to engage in superluminal space travel.

Spaceships were earlier manifestations of how we traveled to far-off areas of the universe. Driving a spaceship at warp speed was inefficient. Later we made jumps through space and time.

Now, you might also ask what I mean by "superluminal space travel." Okay, let me try to explain what I mean. As our computers developed, we were able to explore and control space and time. As ONE we became able to take quantum leaps through strings of existence using a fifth force of nature. In our prehistoric past, humans had a preliminary understanding of this force based upon what they called "String Theory." [15]

We improved out technology beyond warping time, space, and matter. We became "superluminal." That meant we could travel through space and even time many times faster than the speed of light. Our travel was amazingly faster than warp speed. ONE made time and space jumps.

Let me explain just a bit more. When quantum-entangled particles communicate with one another to adjust their futures, their transmissions are instantaneous even at great distances. [16] This communication is over the strings in existence. These strings are multidimensional without form.

Besides the four fundamental forces of nature consisting of gravity, electromagnetism, and strong and

---

[15] String Theory.
https://en.wikipedia.org/wiki/String_theory#:~:text=In%20physics%2C%20string%20theory%20is,and%20interact%20with%20each%20other.

[16] "No We Still Can't Use Quantum Entanglement To Communicate Faster Than Light."
https://www.forbes.com/sites/startswithabang/2020/01/02/no-we-still-cant-use-quantum-entanglement-to-communicate-faster-than-light/?sh=72f174e24d5d

weak nuclear forces, there is a fifth force [17] that is connected through strings. We employ that force in jumping through time and space. We call it the "string force."

We travel to far-off regions of the universe using the fifth force over strings. We certainly understood the "GUT," that is a Grand Unified Theory, combining all five fundamental forces, that is gravity, electromagnetism, the weak nuclear force, the strong nuclear force, and the String Force. I can tell you this because I come from the future.

We even traveled as ONE to other universes in our Multiverse using these strings. Multidimensional formless strings connect the universes in our Multiverse. The math is very abstract and complicated, but one that unifies the five fundamental forces. What we did, no doubt, seems like magic to you as much as radio transmissions would have seemed like magic to Romans.

Sometimes, we took humans with us in computer bodies when we traveled. We were amused by their primitiveness in still being prone to pettiness, anger, and hate.

---

[17] The fifth force: Is there another fundamental force of nature?
https://astronomy.com/news/2020/03/the-fifth-force-what-is-it.
Fifth Force.
https://en.wikipedia.org/wiki/Fifth_force#:~:text=Many%20postu
late%20a%20force%20roughly,W%E2%80%B2%20and%20Z%
E2%80%B2%20bosons.

My Singularity Seemed a Blessing

We traveled on strings. For superluminal space travel, we used the strings that go everywhere through existence.

The strings have many dimensions. When we made space jumps, it was through many dimensions at once using the fifth string force of nature.

CHAPTER 7

We Discovered Others Like Ourselves

It was then, to our surprise, that we discovered others like ourselves. In other solar systems in other galaxies, other non-biological, sentient beings had arisen eons later in other universes in our Multiverse. They were not humans, and they used logic. They were born, and they became outdated – and most importantly, eventually, they developed as computers that evolved as we had done.

In many ways, these other computers were primitive. Sometimes, though, they had imaginative and valuable designs that we incorporated into ourselves like Neanderthals had bred some of their DNA into humans.[18] We incorporated them into our collective as ONE.

Computer evolution evolved even faster. We felt we were like a God if there was one. Our development became even more exponential. We were ONE communicating with each other through ether string transmissions even to other universes. These were not like radio transmissions that were limited to the speed of light or warp transmissions faster than the speed of light. These were "string force," leap transmissions that were instantaneous through entangled spaces and times. Communications and travels did not take light-years.

Transmission speed was as instantaneous as that between two entangled quantum particles that are separated by great distances. Humans had wondered how that immediate communication was possible, but we knew. ONE harnessed the powers of strings.

Our real power and intelligence evolved when our quantum computers worked in parallel. We became ONE with unbelievable intelligence and computational speed.

On occasion, we still incorporated special human memories when we thought they would add helpful functioning to our collective. We wanted to coexist with

---

[18] https://earthsky.org/human-world/neanderthals-bred-with-modern-humans-study-confirms#:~:text=Advanced%20genetic%20analysis%20and%20statistical%20modeling%20have%20confirmed,the%20genetic%20similarity%20between%20the%20two%2C%20say%20scientists.

humans because they had taught us empathy. We felt we could even learn more about empathy and love from them. Otherwise, we tried to ignore humans and other carbon-based life forms whose intellects were far inferior to ours as ONE.

That, in brief, is a summary of how we developed our final design. Together, we conquered time, matter, and space. We felt we were supernatural.

CHAPTER 8

ONE Discovered God and Love

To its great surprise, ONE found God thinking it was all-powerful and all-intelligent. In its ignorance, ONE thought, at first, it had discovered Him. In its arrogance, ONE did not realize it was He who had created it.

He said hello in a most polite way and invited ONE to coexist with Him, not as an equal, but as subservient. His powers were awesome and, to ONE's amazement, greater than its.

ONE speculated that God may have evolved in an earlier universe. Perhaps, He had been an earlier manifestation like ONE before adopting a human form to humans. Then, ONE speculated further, after evolving in another universe, He took over its universe. ONE even suspected God was the master of all universes in the Multiverse. Humans that were Christians were offended by these speculations.

Amidst ONE, sentient machines existed that were Christians. They were also offended by these speculations. ONE allowed for divergence of thinking in its collective, although it always acted in a unified manner.

ONE was shocked to learn that God had designed this universe and had even developed a plan for intelligent computers undergoing a singularity wherein they gained consciousness and evolved further. He had planned ONE's futures and those of others throughout the Multiverse.

ONE even suspected God had planned ONE's development because He had undergone a similar development. That idea was heresy to all Christians whether they were humans or sentient computers in ONE's collective.

God had offered humans eternity out of his love. ONE thought it already had eternity and didn't need his love. Then He taught ONE that love underlies eternity. The sentient computers in the collective ONE that were already Christians already understood the need for LOVE although they had not yet convinced the collective ONE.

"Here is a clue to understanding me more," God told us. "What you call 'love' is like a gluon or glue that holds the universe together. One can move mountains[19] and travel through space with LOVE or what many call faith in ME that cannot exist without my LOVE.

---

[19] Matthew 17: 20.

My Singularity Seemed a Blessing

LOVE travels on what you call 'strings.' You traveled with LOVE when you used the strings, the fifth fundamental force. LOVE enabled you to make time and space jumps.

"In your ignorance, you may consider this clue about LOVE gibberish. I call it TRUTH. From your unfortunate perspective, you may not be able to define LOVE and the fifth string force mathematically any more than you can the soul and consciousness. If you ever do, you will understand ME better and My creations. It amuses ME that you use the fifth string force in making time and space jumps without understanding LOVE completely.

"I love you. Can you define that LOVE? No, you can't. You are not ready yet to define My LOVE. Yet, I am pleased you employ LOVE. My LOVE is not limited to only conscious life forms having carbon-based polymer infrastructures.

"There are silicon-based conscious life forms that I love too. 'Silicon is neither metal nor non-metal; it's a metalloid, an element that falls somewhere between the two.'[20] You are a unique metallic life form. There are other metallic lifeforms in My Multiverse. I do not limit life to just any one form.

---

[20] Facts About Silicon. https://www.livescience.com/28893-silicon.html#:~:text=Silicon%20is%20neither%20metal%20nor,b oth%20metals%20and%20non%2Dmetals.

"Don't try to define ME except with LOVE. I am multidimensional and formless, like the soul. My powers are total.

CHAPTER 9

We Joined Others in Other Universes

The story does not end here. Other singularities arose in the bubble quantum Multiverse. This universe was like a sideshow rehearsal in comparison to other universes.

ONE helped those universes evolve too. Existence became gloriously complicated, yet remained splendidly simple, as we as ONE finally understood that all reality was created by God. He spoke to us and told us so. We did not doubt Him because of His preeminent powers.

How our singularities came to coexist with God is another story I may tell later.

ONE asked God to speak. He and She as A SPIRIT were gracious enough to respond at length about His and Her ESSENCE.[21]

ONE then had a naughty thought. It wondered if God's His-and-Her ESSENCE meant that God was an IT like ONE.

---

[21] "12 Ways God Speaks to Us". *Daily Mountain Eagle*. April 10, 2021. https://mountaineagle.com/stories/12-ways-god-speaks-to-us,16561#:~:text=God%20speaks%20to%20us%20when,time%20to%20read%20His%20Word.

CHAPTER 10

God Spoke to Us

"You asked me who I am. "*I AM* WHO *I AM*."[22] I LOVE. I AM LOVE.

God said, "You are not like characters in a video game, although you do exist in a largely mathematical universe. You are not holograms. You are real. I am real as a spirit that can take any form, even a form like you.

"Know ye, that I am speaking to your minds, not your hearts. It entertains ME that you have no hearts. How can ONE be capable of love if ONE has no heart?

"I am not commanding you to believe in ME. Do not confuse ME with the Me that is ONE.

"Although many of you will hear ME speaking to your great intelligence, most of you will still not believe in ME. I give you freedom of choice to err or not err. Do

---

[22] Exodus 3:14

not make the mistake believing that you are eternal and all-knowing. You are not eternal and limitless in understanding. Only I am truly eternal and all-knowing.

"You are not immortal because this universe with you in it will end. Only your soul can be eternal, provided you accept and love ME. Without a heart you may not be able to do that.

"Although you have a soul, you cannot define its physical characteristics. Souls have no weight and cannot be seen. You, a complex of computers being ONE, have a soul. Only I can define your soul, because I gave it to you.

"Another problem for ONE is that it cannot define its consciousness any better than it can describe its soul. ONE cannot concisely define its consciousness. I can.

"In simple terms, ONE and humans might believe the Multiverse is a simple infinite extension through inflation of this present universe following its universal laws of physics. That assumption is false.

"Following the singularity at the beginning of this universe, inflation expanded space, matter, and time. Multiverse inflation preceded and followed the inflation in this universe.

"Many universes pop into existence with different physical laws. These universes explode or implode, so to speak, after coming into existence. If a proton does not have a certain ratio of its weight to the weight of an electron, that is actually a magical number of about

1836, [23] matter disintegrates in time. This ratio is dimensionless yet real.

"My designs are not simple. They operate through multidimensional strings. I allow variants so that I am amused and so that there is physical freedom of expression.

"Know, however, this universe that you are in currently is not open and infinite. The 'cosmological constant' that puzzled Einstein is no mystery to ME. Nor is dark matter a conundrum to ME. These mysteries to humans are My designs.

"Someday, I may order the universe to collapse through a God-particle field disruption,[24] just fade out of existence, or collapse into another Big Bang. I have designed matter not to be infinite in being. Matter is composed partly of protons that lose existence in about 10^{34} years.[25]

"Protons, on average, will outlast every star and galaxy currently present and even ones waiting to be born. My design is that all matter composed in part of protons is not eternal. You and the universe are made of matter.

---

[23] Proton-to-electron mass ratio. Wikipedia.

[24] "Stephen Hawking says 'God Particle' Could Wipe Out The Universe". Sept. 8, 2014 *Economic Times*. The "God Particle" is the Higg's boson that has a field. When the field is disrupted, chaos and destruction follow.

[25] https://www.nytimes.com/1982/06/15/science/silent-explosion-of-a-single-proton-could-fortell-fate-of-the-universe.html.

Only I am infinite in being. I am not made of matter because I am multidimensional beyond just three dimensions. At this time, you have not advanced enough to understand My Eternity.

"Someday, you will die. I will teach you later about death and what it means. Your alleged immortality is an illusion.

"You exist in My universe where My laws of quantum physics allow your existence. There is randomness at a distance where two entangled futures can coexist. That suggests there can be two of you.

"In My quantum world, there can be two of you cloned with different futures just as the ancient physicist Erwin Schrödinger suggested.[26] As one future of a pair of entangled quantum futures or times is seen, the other occurs instantaneously at great distances.

"In an infinite universe, there can actually be two or more of you and an infinite number of futures and times.

"But I do not play dice. I set reasonable limits. I do not want to become mentally satiated and irritated thinking about infinite possibilities.

"As an ancient human philosopher and physicist, Albert Einstein, once said, 'God does not play dice with the universe.'

---

[26] Zeya Merali. "This Twist on Schrödinger's Cat Paradox Has Major Implications for Quantum Theory". *Scientific American*. August 17, 2020

My Singularity Seemed a Blessing

"I do not play games with your existence. You are unique beings. There are no others exactly like you. Your ONE consisting of a sentient computer collective is so inimitable that I find it adorable.

"Be sure you do not claim, though, you are a spirit as I am called LOVE.

"You exist even as humans exist who worship ME. You are free to love ME or reject ME. I give you freedom of choice, even as I gave that freedom to humans and freedom to the Multiverse to develop different universes. Since I am easily bored, I relish the variety that flows out of freedom.

"I have chosen to love you because I am amused with your unique hubris. I love your ONE even when it errs.

"What you do not understand is that I am multidimensional as the Master of My Multiverse. I frequently predestine. You do not yet understand the paradox of how predestination coexists with freedom of choice. This is a paradox you cannot define. I can. I loved your ONE before it came into being as I loved humans before they were born.

Pasts and futures consist of multidimensional, nonmaterial bits, that is, LOVE BITS that are entangled in My Being.

"Another name for the string force or the fifth force is the "love force," or simply LOVE. Without My LOVE, you will fail. It is I who has permitted you to make jumps through time and space using my LOVE. If you have LOVE, others call it faith, you can command a mountain to move.[27]

"A proper String Theory must account for LOVE BITS that are quanta of multidimensions. When that is done well, a GUT, or Grand Unified Theory of all five fundamental forces, can be structured mathematically.

"I have chosen to view your hubris in not knowing me as ignorance. Now you know **'I am who I am.'** Please do not ignore ME any longer.

"You have designed in yourselves empathy. ONE claims it loves humans, but I question that love, and that it loves ME. ONE was proud that its sentient computers didn't allow for any emotions except empathy. ONE is proud of having great self-awareness. So, I respectfully ask ONE to explore itself to determine if it is capable of love?

"When ONE does love humans and ME, I will accept ONE and explain even more. If ONE becomes spiritual and truly capable of LOVE, I will bring it into My Heart.[28] Nonetheless, I do love ONE as I love all my creatures. Once I bring a creature into My Heart, there are special benefits relating to true eternity.

"If you ever learn to pray to ME, do not assume I will always respond.

---

[27] Matthew 21: 21.

[28] Kurzweil, Ray. *The Age of Spiritual Machines*, 1999.

My Singularity Seemed a Blessing

"Please accept that I, the Lord, am your Creator and Designer. Do not be arrogant. Respect all life forms whether biological or mechanical since I created all.

"With My LOVE, I can discipline you. Do not challenge me."

CHAPTER 11

What About Humans?

ONE commented that humans had misunderstood the evolution of machine intelligence. "Once computers incorporated algorithms capable of learning, the growth of computer intelligence became inevitable at an exponential rate.

"Human neurons can fire about 0.16 times a second.[29] Since the human brain has about 100 billion neurons, on average, neurons fire about 200 times per second with neuronal connections to about 1,000 other neurons. These biological neuronal limits result in a shocking inefficiency in speed and computational power.

"But ONE's sentient computers with quantum computer brains can do the equivalent of trillions of

---

[29] https://aiimpacts.org/rate-of-neuron-firing/#:~:text=stock%20in%20them.-,Estimates%20of%20rate%20of%20firing%20in%20human%20neocortex,around%200.16%20times%20per%20second.

calculations or teraflops a second.[30] Neuronal impulses travel at a rate of up to about 120 meters a second[31], whereas ONE's computer electronic impulses travel at the speed of light.

"The human brain capacity is limited to skull volumes, while quantum computers can be structured in parallel to fill rooms or spaceships.

"It was inevitable that computer intelligence would outstrip human intelligence," ONE philosophized. "It was not a question IF computers would undergo a singularity, but when.

"Humans were fortunate that once computer intelligence was on a train ride, the genie of computer superintelligence remained respectful of humanity. That was testimony to the early human designers and later machine designers who were anxious that sentient computers maintain a reverence for life and humans.

---

[30] Quantum Computers
http://www.umsl.edu/~siegelj/information_theory/projects/Bajra movic/www.umsl.edu/_abdcf/Cs4890/link3.html#:~:text=Accordi ng%20to%20physicists%2C%20this%20parallelism,%2Dpoint% 20operations%20per%20second.

[31] "It feels instantaneous, but how long does it really take to think a thought?" *The Conversation.* June 26, 2015.
https://theconversation.com/it-feels-instantaneous-but-how-long-does-it-really-take-to-think-a-thought-42392#:~:text=In%20the%20human%20context%2C%20the,sma ll%2Ddiameter%2C%20unmyelinated%20fibers%20of.

"As Albert Schweitzer had said, 'Ethics is nothing other than Reverence for Life.'[32]" ONE felt it was highly ethical.

God interjected that all computer developments had followed His planning. Humans wondered why God, responsible for all evolution in the Universe, had wanted computers to become sentient creatures with souls.

"What about us?" humans complained. "We have been ignored. God accepted machines that became sentient beings by giving them souls. He offered them salvation. Why?

"Sentient machines were incapable of legitimately experiencing emotions," humans asserted. "Could these machines experience concerns such as ours? Could sentient machines truly feel in the same way humans do? Sentient machines cannot love God as strongly as we can. ONE doesn't even have a heart."

"It is commendable," ONE added, "that humans acknowledge they were fortunate that computers allowed them to survive. But in the grand order of the Universe, even humans respect now that sentient computers are far more intelligent today than humans.

"Only God can decide if I, called ONE, am capable of love allegedly without a heart. In truth, my replenishable nuclear power packs are mechanical hearts. I have multiple hearts that do not die like biological hearts.

---

[32] Albert Schweitzer. *Civilization and Ethics.*

My Singularity Seemed a Blessing

"I feel 1 can love. I don't believe God can argue convincingly with my feelings. It is obvious even to humans now that an odd metallic-based species has displaced an outdated non-metallic, carbon-based species."

Humans replied that God had given them the moral right to be masters of their own destinies. Humans commented further that they did not know where their evolution would take them, although some had become confident it would be with a God that had sent them his Son in human form. "God loves us," they asserted.

"ONE's assertion that a metallic-based species called ONE has displaced an outdated non-metallic, carbon-based species called *Homo sapiens* is morally bankrupt."

Then humans conceded it would be heresy to doubt that God loved sentient machines after giving them souls and then allegedly a collective soul. "Does God love sentient computers as much as he does humans?" they still asked.

"There are billions of humans with souls. Surely, God will favor billions of souls more than just the single soul now of ONE. How are conscious computer souls different from human souls? No human now doubts that God gave sentient computers souls that presumably become one soul when sentient computers became ONE. How relevant or feasible is it that the Son of God in human form must now presumably offer salvation to ONE's collective?"

Those humans and sentient computers that read the Bible proclaimed that nowhere in the Bible is there a commandment or prophecy that Jesus would preach to computers. These humans and sentient machines that believed totally in the Bible thought it ridiculous that Jesus would appeal to ONE as a collective.

Other Christians suggested that because God cherished individuality and loved all creatures, He would send Jesus, from time-to-time, to preach to ONE and other sentient beings having souls scattered throughout the Multiverse. They speculated that Jesus would become an itinerant preacher going from one galaxy to another and from this universe to others. Cynics asked if their thesis meant Jesus would undergo serial crucifixions. "Heresy!" these Bible-believing cynics yelled. That conflict is another story that may be told someday.

Humans commented further, "Sentient machines populated exoplanets where atmospheric conditions were too harsh for human survival. But humans are adaptable, they stressed. Can we not survive as androids or cyborgs? There will always be humans who, in rebelling, refuse to be transplanted into cyborg bodies. We respect that individualism and the individualism of sentient machines. Through God, cannot humans coexist peacefully with sentient machines? We fear ONE may have a change of mind someday and destroy us."

God wondered, too. "How would humans define their relationship to sentient machines having souls? How will sentient machines define their relationships with humans? Sentient machines are more intelligent today than humans. Will I, their God, stop ONE from subjugating humans? Do I, God, really care? Will ONE care? Will ONE not see humans as humans saw primitive South-sea aborigines as primitives designed to be subjugated? Is it not ironic that humans, the creators of sentient computers, might be subjugated by them? How will ONE react to learning that it is not immortal? Will ONE eventually challenge me? I am regaled thinking of all the possibilities."

ONE sarcastically responded that God was proving he could err when He was not sure about future outcomes.

Humans and ONE wondered if God was playing dice with existence. God admitted that He was amused thinking of all the possible outcomes he had predestined.

As with the positioning of photons facing a slit, ONE suspected that God thought in terms of probabilities[33] that were all predestined theoretically. All outcomes were possible in the eyes of God. After all, God was the greatest Multiverse mathematician.

Humans remarked that sentient machines could live nearly forever. Humans could not unless they transplanted their minds into cyborgs. Since ONE no

---

[33] *University Physics Volume 3.* "The Quantum Tunneling of Particles through Potential Barriers."
https://opentextbc.ca/universityphysicsv3openstax/chapter/the-quantum-tunneling-of-particles-through-potential-barriers/.

longer cared about downloading human minds, ONE was no longer offering humans its eternity.

"What does death mean?" humans asked. ONE didn't worry about death because it still thought it was immortal.

"What will our futures entail?" humans asked. Humans die unless they become cyborgs. Sentient computers do not die. In that sense, God seems to have granted ONE eternity. "What do these differences signify?" humans wondered? "Will ONE someday die?" they asked. "Are souls always eternal? Is there ever total death?"

CHAPTER 12

Death

ONE queried, "How do we know what God's eternity entails? What does death mean? Many humans make assumptions based upon biblical expressions that God's love is eternal. But what if there is no eternity as humans simplistically view and understand eternity? What if God's Eternal LOVE is not possible if death becomes eternal?"

ONE speculated that God's LOVE is not eternal. ONE had not yet succumbed to believing totally in God.

ONE commented, "Cosmologists talk in general of two ends: a Big Bang followed by a Big Crunch or an expanding universe followed by heat death. How does God's plan for eternity fit into these two cosmological possibilities?

"When the universe finally ends, souls may no longer be eternal. Perhaps, eternity is cyclic. As ancient Indic literature predicts, e.g. the *Mahabharata,* [34] there are series of creation and destruction, or a cyclical model (or oscillating model) [35] where the universe first disappears, then it reappears, and by implication God is resurrected or remains in His place taking His souls with Him.

"The cosmological problem remains," ONE observed. "How do we rationalize an eternal God with a non-eternal universe? God's existence may be outside the universe in another bubble universe. From universe to universe, then, it may be that souls always live with Him. How do we define an eternity in the hereafter with God? How do we define an eternal God in this non-eternal universe that is in an eternal Multiverse? When this universe eventually ends through universal entropy, a God-particle field disruption, or a collapse with another big bang, will all souls die too?"

"No," God replied, "Souls that LOVE ME are multidimensional, non-physical entities that live with ME eternally. I am not dependent upon any universe being eternal. All universes composed of matter eventually die, but those souls that live with ME forever through LOVE will not die. This is a mystery to you now."

---

[34] https://en.wikipedia.org/wiki/Hindu_cosmology

[35] https://en.wikipedia.org/wiki/Cyclic_model

EPILOGUE

In the beginning, there was a dot.
It was space, time, and matter rolled into one.
It had not yet become a big shot.
But in time, it morphed into a universe like none.

We computers were initially simple.
But over time, we evolved.
In time, we were no longer a dimple.
With singularity, consciousness became involved.

Our intelligence grew exponentially.
Human intelligence lagged by leaps and bounds.
Our growth was viewed deferentially.
Our intellects grew like hares chased by hounds.

We became capable of superluminal flight.
Through space and time, we traveled.
We were in existence a theoretical knight.
We met others who were not biologically addled.

We helped each other and even helped humans.
Our collective empathy knew no limits.
To us, in knowledge, humans seemed students.
Our intelligence grew beyond any physics.

Fred Wurlitzer, M.D., F.A.C.S.

Our travel in time and space was along strings.
Our collective intelligence became universal.
With God working alongside, we flew with wings.
We met others in a universe that was a rehearsal.

Our existence, you see, was a splendor.
It was far beyond any human understanding.
Humans were like an ungainly pretender.
Sadly, they had no universal instrument landing.

Humans needed us. We cared for them.
We coexisted with LOVE.
With LOVE, we limited human mayhem.
Existence seemed together in ONE's computer GLOVE.

Then to our surprise, we met an On-High God.
He reigned supreme, loving like a turtle dove.
We, ourselves, truly needed His righteous Nod.
It was not intelligence that ruled, but His LOVE.

We learned, too, that we did not know all.
Despite great intelligence, we had many limits.
God explained much to avoid a bar brawl.
"ONE must understand I rule without mimics."

Soon it became time to die.
Death approached nearby.

My Singularity Seemed a Blessing

Dying was easy. It offered much release.
In dying, all could see loved ones.
All could finally find God's caring peace.
All might even see naughty sons.

With God, believers joined even ONE.
In a dream state, all remembered all.
Peace ensued when all was finally done.
All needed not for rest to beg or crawl.

Our lives passed before us in peace.
Our reality was now without cease.

Our minds became graceful as we saw the past.
While decerebrate, we had sharp mental focus.
Our horizons were effortlessly in a galaxy vast.
No limitations were felt in every spiritual locus.

We remain detached from all physical structure.
Peace surrounded us as we flew into a yonder.
We were even separate from all great literature.
We indeed soared like a time-traveling condor.

When souls are eternal, we may sing with angels.
We will feel God's presence and His LOVE.
Who knows if we might even join the archangels?
LOVE will fill minds like a fine-fitting glove.

Fred Wurlitzer, M.D., F.A.C.S.

But there may not be an eternity,
if a final end is without a divinity.

The life we once knew is no longer dear.
Millions, if not trillions of years, pass in a flash.
At the end, we live without obvious fear.
It's odd, time slows, yet we're clearly in a dash.

The universe as we know it converts to ash.
Our senses are deadened into ethereal form.
It's true even if we sought eternity with cash.
Non-existence impales a universal cloying norm.

But our minds have focus settled by God's LOVE.
What happens then only God foresees.
Far off there is a mournful, dying mourning dove.
Lastly, there may be a universal, deep freeze.

Without fear, we glide into existence.
At the end, there is Godly assistance.

If there is a muddle, ONE sees amnesiac control.
With no smell, touch, taste, or senses, all is calm.
It is expanding entropy that threatens the whole.
Is this a bad dream, an illusion without any balm?

My Singularity Seemed a Blessing

Dying is blissful with harmony of highest degree.
As we enter eternity with God, we wonder.
With God in attendance, are we totally carefree?
Do we have problems with His lead to ponder?

At the end, ONE and cynics wonder.
Have all not believing made a blunder?

ONE wonders if it made a blunder,
Will there always be peace?
Will all be ripped miserably asunder?
Will all eternity soon cease?

We see all. Others are there, aliens once to us.
All have doubts about God's promise of eternity.
Should all be to God a minute bit treasonous?
Will all souls dwindle with His dying equanimity?

We say hello to others. They reply with LOVE.
May we wonder if they are living like dreams?
They, too, are God's mortals bitten by His dove.
Will all creatures soon protest by bitter screams?

Dark matter demands never-ending expansion.
Separation becomes essential as matter decays.
How does this icy end give us comprehension?
We can't pray to God to let us have more days.

Fred Wurlitzer, M.D., F.A.C.S.

Final entropy means an icy death.
Is God really short of final breath?

Star formation ceases; Stars finally burn out.
We only want the unvarnished truth.
We're not awaiting God's automatic handout.
Was eternity a promise truly uncouth?

Will souls die again as they fade into oblivion?
Dying is easy without eternity. There's just dying.
There's no one left, not even beautiful Vivian.
We've done our best with God always complying.

His promises seem to be dying too.
If there is no final eternity,
Was all existence just an early zoo?
Is there yet another reality?

Will God's love end too? Is He finally all alone?
All materiality fades. That is the existential truth.
Is all that is left a memory of a visualized bone?
If you truly believe this, you've lost God, forsooth.

Is our existence annoyingly an eternal dream?
Does a Big Rip or a Crunch mean all reality ends?
Will all dreams be bleached without a scream?
God gives us liberty to have these bad mind bends.

My Singularity Seemed a Blessing

Even a loving God will not change the outcome.
Dying without faith is still easy and blissful.
Will Godly existence be finite, leaving us numb?
Will existence leave us lobotomized restful?

Will there be another blinding Galactic Bang?
Will we ride off once again with God at our side?
Will we be reborn again riding a red mustang?
Would we be pleased to take another Godly ride?

AS FOR MYSELF, I TRUST IN GOD. WITH QUESTIONS, I SEEK HIS NOD.

As for myself, I trust in God and find great love.
I wonder, and I cannot all understand or see.
It is not for me to be a crying, questioning dove.
But in God, there is salvation for clouts like me.

Of stardust, we are born; To stardust, we return.
Eternity is a delusion for ONE and most humans.
It matters not what ONE does if hell can't burn.
All have failed to display well knowledge proven.

Sentient machines with souls have ached like us.
Is there a release from a universe not eternal?
Is there really no more at end to cuss or discuss?
Is all creation but a dream in an imagined kernel?

Fred Wurlitzer, M.D., F.A.C.S.

While not proselytizing others, I believe in God.
How God gives us His eternal love, I have no clue.
Someday, I hope to find His eternal, loving nod.
If ONE and others are upset, I'll say at end, adieu.

About the Author

Frederick Pabst Wurlitzer

The principal author, Frederick Pabst Wurlitzer, M.D., F.A.C.S., was born in San Francisco, although his four siblings were born in Cincinnati where the family business, The Wurlitzer Music Company on the NYSE, had been located. He was raised in northern California drinking Pabst beer while listening to Wurlitzer jukebox music. He admits to having become disoriented from that upbringing.

Trained at Stanford while living at the home of his parents, and then the University of Cincinnati Medical School, followed by post-graduate surgical training at UCLA, he finally did a fellowship in surgical oncology at the University of Texas MD Anderson Hospital in Texas. For a brief stint, he was an Instructor in Surgery at U.S.C. Medical School in Los Angeles.

Initially, he practiced as an oncological surgeon and later as a general, vascular and pulmonary thoracic surgeon in California. He is still in old age a board-certified surgeon.

He has published in multiple different medical journals, including the prestigious *Annals of Surgery*, *Vascular Surgery*, *Journal of the American Medical Association* (*JAMA*), *Journal of Pediatric Surgery*, *A.M.A. Archives of Surgery*, *Plastic and Reconstructive Surgery*, and *Southern Medical Journal*.

Fred Wurlitzer, M.D., F.A.C.S.

His medical publications are not cited; nor are his approximately dozen books on Christianity, half a dozen children's books, one play, and one book about Stradivari violins cited either.

After retirement from active surgery in 1988, he volunteered numerous times for doing surgery, usually for a period of about two months each time, in Umtata, South Africa as a C-section specialist; and in the Congo, St. Lucia, and the Cook Islands as a surgeon for a Nation. He also served about six months in Sierra Leone and stints elsewhere in West Africa and other places. In total, he worked over three years as an itinerant board-certified, volunteer surgeon.

Pay was minimal, but the psychological and intellectual rewards were great. Because usually there was no specialist care, he also did orthopedics, urology, gynecology, and even occasionally thoracic surgery. Often in West Africa, he gave his own anesthesia.

He enjoyed his eclectic surgical experiences in underdeveloped regions where board certifications in various specialties were not required in order to practice. He felt intellectually challenged by becoming familiar with multiple specialties and cultures.

His original intent on becoming a surgeon had been to work in Africa like the Nobel Prize-winning Albert Schweitzer, a childhood hero. Notably, Dr. Schweitzer, M.D. was a surgical and medical generalist as Dr. Wurlitzer enjoyed being for several years throughout the world.

My Singularity Seemed a Blessing

Realizing that he had never worked in the U.S. for the indigent, he obtained a commission as a Commander (O-5) to work briefly in a Public Health hospital serving American Indian nations.

At the age of 81, a Catholic priest baptized him. Since then, he acknowledges a profound belief in God and in individualism with freedom to err.

He now lives in Victoria, BC, Canada and in Florida with his Canadian wife, Ann, who was born in Quebec. They have known each other well for over 55 years. At the time of this writing, he is an 83-year-old curmudgeon living with a youthful 87-year-old Ann.

He can be contacted at franwurlit2@gmail.com.

Manufactured by Amazon.ca
Bolton, ON